POLAR
THE TITANIC BEAR

by DAISY CORNING STONE SPEDDEN
Illustrations by LAURIE MCGAW

I discovered this story about a little boy and his toy bear among the belongings of one of my relatives, Daisy Corning Stone Spedden. It is a true story that Daisy wrote for her only son, Douglas. Douglas adored "Polar," his beautiful white mohair bear, and took him everyplace he went. When the Spedden family stepped onto the *Titanic* in April 1912, Douglas and Polar never dreamed that they would soon be part of the most famous sea disaster of all time.

— *Leighton H. Coleman III*

A MADISON PRESS BOOK
produced for
LITTLE, BROWN AND COMPANY

"That's my tenth bear today," said the voice of a young woman proudly. Suddenly I felt myself being hurled through the air, then landing with a thump on a hard wooden bench. I opened my eyes and looked around the large, bright room littered with sawdust, tools and scraps of felt. On either side of a long table sat women who were quickly sewing black glass eyes onto teddy bears. I soon learned that they earned their living by making bears and other stuffed animals for toy shops around the world. Christmas was approaching, and they had been given a large order. This special lot of bears, including me, was to be shipped from Germany to America.

I wondered where America was and how I was to get there, but I didn't have long to wait.

The next morning, I was crammed into a box, my toes touching my ears. Weeks passed in darkness, as I was jostled this way and that. First there was the rumbling of the baggage train, then the swaying of the ship, then the shouts of the dockhands.

But I forgot about my aching limbs when a young woman lifted me out of my box and set me on a shelf with a dozen other bears. She dusted us all off and then tied blue or pink ribbons around our necks. I had arrived at F.A.O. Schwarz, in New York, the largest toy shop in the world.

I was amazed by the beautiful things I could see from my perch. From the ceiling hung every sort of flying machine — airships, aeroplanes and hot-air balloons. In a long case in front of me were little furnishings for dolls' houses — tiny bird cages, baby carriages, and bathtubs with china dolls in them. There was a wonderful railway worked by electricity, and I could see a bright red engine going around and around, past flashing signal towers and stations.

A 1910 postcard of F.A.O. Schwarz's main store.

An old advertisement for F.A.O. Schwarz.

Because it was Christmastime, the shop was busy every day. My bear companions disappeared one by one, and I couldn't help wondering when my turn would come.

One day a lady with red cheeks looked me all over carefully, straightened my blue bow, and said she would take me along with her. I was sad to leave my lovely surroundings and hated being packed into a horrid little box again by one of the salesclerks.

For several days I was left in a closet. I thought everyone had forgotten me, but finally one morning the lady took me out of the box. Then we went down to the docks where we boarded a large ship called the *Caronia*.

Douglas's mother stands with some friends on the deck of the Caronia.

The decks of the ship were crowded with people saying good-bye. As I looked about wondering what was to become of me, a little boy came running up.

Flinging his arms around the lady with the red cheeks, he cried, "Oh, Aunt Nannie, I wish you were coming with us!"

She gave him a big hug and then presented me to him. The little boy, my new master, had his father and mother with him and Nurse Burns, whom he called "Muddie Boons." Several people came down to see Master's family off, and I was admired by each one in turn, which made me feel very proud.

"How high he holds his head!" Master's father said. "What will you call him?"

"Polar," Master replied promptly.

Reid's Palace Hotel was one of the finest places to stay in Madeira.

Tennis and walks around the harbor were part of a visit to the island.

A week later, we sighted the island of Madeira, near Portugal, which was to be our home for the next few months. It was a beautiful bright afternoon when we went ashore. We traveled through the busy streets to our hotel in a rickety old wooden cart pulled by a bull.

Our hotel was very grand. Master, Muddie Boons and I had a big sunny room overlooking the garden and the blue sea beyond.

I spent many lazy days out under the palms watching Master build little houses with sticks and stones and surround them with miniature gardens. And we rode in the bullock carts whenever we went up into the hills, exploring different parts of the island.

One sad day, Master woke up with red spots all over his face. "He's got measles," the doctor said gravely. "You'll have to put him in quarantine." Everyone looked very worried.

Master, Muddie Boons and I were moved to a little cottage a short distance from the hotel. Master's mother explained that being in "quarantine" meant staying away from the other guests so that we wouldn't give them measles.

We weren't in our new home for five minutes before a big brown mouse scampered across the floor. Poor Muddie Boons shrieked and went after it with a broom. She soon named our cottage "Mouse Castle" because it was full of mice, rats and ants, and she spent all her spare minutes trying to kill them. I didn't like my new quarters a bit, for Master was too sick to even notice me, and I was put in a corner and forgotten.

The doctor visited us often, and every day Master's parents came with fresh eggs and milk. Night after night, I watched as Muddie

Muddie Boons in "Mouse Castle."

Boons sat awake, holding Master's hot, limp hand in hers. A full week passed, and I began to wonder if he would ever be well enough to play with me again.

But one morning, I heard Master ask for me in a faint little voice. Muddie Boons handed me to him, and he put me on his pillow, and there I lay without stirring the whole day.

Slowly, Master began to grow stronger. He would sit up in bed, wash my face and paws, tie my ribbon and give me my breakfast. I was so happy to see him better that I almost didn't care what he did to me. But I didn't relish the bath Muddie Boons gave me one morning in a horrid, smelly liquid called disinfectant. She gave Master one, too. Then two men came to the garden with a hammock. They carefully lifted Master in as he held tight to his little American flag in one hand and me in the other. Muddie Boons led the way, and we all marched back to our own sunny room in the hotel.

Douglas is carried back to the hotel, where he rests on the balcony.

Soon Douglas is well enough to sit up. Here he is seen with the doctor and Muddie Boons.

Early in April, we sailed back to America on a ship called the *Adriatic*. After we arrived in New York, we went to Master's new home in Tuxedo Park, which was surrounded by trees and overlooked a little lake.

When the weather turned hot and sticky, we went to the family's summer house near Bar Harbor, Maine. I enjoyed splashing in the ocean with Master or sitting on the rocks while he built forts and castles. Once he forgot about me, and the tide came in and almost carried me out to sea, but luckily Master rescued me just in time.

When winter came, we returned to Tuxedo Park. Master and I tumbled about in the snow and made snowmen. Best of all he gave me rides on his sled, running as fast as he could across the ice-covered lake while the cold wind whistled in my ears.

At Christmas I had my own tree and new toys to play with. I enjoyed a delicious turkey dinner served on a small table that Master made for me.

Polar sits at his own table for Christmas dinner in Tuxedo Park.

*Douglas and his
family saw these huge locks
being built for the Panama Canal.*

In the new year we sailed away to some hot, sunny places. We went to Panama, where a great canal was being built right through the country so that ships could sail from one side to the other. One of the engineers invited Master, Muddie Boons and me to ride out to see it in his big private car. Bright flocks of parrots flew from the trees as we roared down the jungle roads.

Bermuda was our last stop. Master took me to a beautiful beach where we

Douglas and his mother in Bermuda.

spent many a long afternoon. He would make a sort of throne out of sand for me to sit on and say, "Now, Polar, don't you run away, but just stay quiet while I work."

So I sat there watching him play and sniffing the salt air.

The next winter we once more set sail on the *Caronia*, this time for Algiers, in northern Africa. The weather was sunny, so we spent our days on deck romping about with the other children. The captain and Master were great friends, and we were often invited to his room for a cup of "tea," as Master called his hot water and sugar.

In Algiers we saw Arabs dressed in long flowing robes. We stayed in a big hotel with a garden, where I would sit on a bench with Muddie Boons while Master played ball.

In February we celebrated George Washington's birthday. Master invited a few friends. We decorated the table with American flags, and Master dressed in red, white and blue. After our tea party we all fished presents from a big bag!

A postcard showing the square in Algiers.

Douglas and his father in the hotel garden.

These postcards show scenes of Monte Carlo and Cannes in 1912.

From Algiers we set sail for the south coast of France. At Monte Carlo, we rode to our hotel on the hill in a funny narrow railway. Master told me it was a funicular railway and that it was pulled along by a cable.

Then we went to Cannes where we stayed for nearly a month. I sat in the hotel garden every morning while Master had an hour's spelling lesson with Muddie Boons.

One day we heard a loud buzzing noise.

"An aeroplane!" Master shouted, throwing down his books.

"Goodness me!" Muddie Boons cried, jumping to her feet. We all craned our necks up to the sky and watched as the aeroplane circled overhead. I could see the pilot sitting in the cockpit with his goggles on, and he waved at us before heading out over the sea.

We took the night train to Paris. Strolling in the Tuileries Gardens, we saw boys sailing their boats in the fountains and watched hot-air balloons rising toward the sky. Master took me partway up the Eiffel Tower one day

and told me it was 984 feet high. He was always telling me the height and length of things.

I was sorry when it was time to go back to America, for I loved Paris. But Master was excited because we were to sail to New York on the *Titanic*, a magnificent new ship. Everyone said she was the biggest ship in the world. We were going to be on her very first voyage. The *Titanic* had left England

A postcard of the Titanic *and one of the ship's diamond-shaped luggage stickers.*

The Nomadic *carried the family out to the* Titanic.

the day before and her first stop was at Cherbourg, France. We took a train to Cherbourg and that evening went out to the huge ship on a little tugboat.

As we stepped on board, the ship's doctor, who had known all of us on the *Adriatic*, kissed Master and said, "I see you still have Polar with you, little man!"

We had fairly smooth weather those first few days and spent most of our time on deck, where Master would spin his whip top or play ball. But we also loved exploring the great ship. There was a giant staircase with a big glass dome over it.

Trying out the rowing machine and the mechanical camel in the ship's gymnasium.

The Grand Staircase.

Master sent me flying down the banister one morning. In the ship's gymnasium, we saw bicycles and rowing machines and even a mechanical camel for the passengers to ride on.

There was a lovely sun parlor on the upper deck where we spent our afternoons, and Master allowed a little girlfriend of his to play with me. We ate in the first-class dining saloon. The tables there were covered with stiffly starched white tablecloths and polished silver, and the ship's band played for us every night. And our stateroom was even bigger than Master's bedroom at home!

One day Master's mother and Muddie Boons went down to the lower decks and had a Turkish bath. They didn't like this hot steam bath one bit, although they did enjoy a cooling dip in the ship's swimming pool afterwards.

No. 659

WHITE STAR LINE.

R.M.S. "TITANIC."

This ticket entitles bearer to use of Turkish or Electric Bath on one occasion.

Paid 4/- or 1 Dollar.

I t was our fifth night at sea. I had been in bed a few hours when I suddenly opened my eyes. The lights had been turned on. Muddie Boons was dressing Master in a great hurry.

After a Turkish steam bath, passengers could cool off in the elegant room shown above or jump into the Titanic's pool.

"Come, we're taking a trip to see the stars," she said. Master's parents were already dressed. They were gathering a few belongings together. I was surprised when I saw Master's mother reach for lifebelts. Then, seizing me from my little net rack beside Master's bed, she tucked me under his arm. We soon joined a group of people standing in the main hall.

Everyone was very quiet, talking in hushed voices. Someone whispered that we had struck an iceberg and that water was pouring into the ship. A young man in uniform helped fasten on Master's lifebelt. Patting him on the head, he said, "Good-bye, little man."

Then Master's father told us to follow him to the top deck, where we would climb into one of the lifeboats.

The lifeboat was swinging out from the ship's side, and people had difficulty climbing aboard. Our little party kept together, and when there were about forty of us in the boat, an officer cried, "Lower away," and we were let down to the water in awful jerks. Master clasped me in his arms. His eyes were shut tight, and his face was white. We finally reached the water safely and rowed off toward a faint light on the horizon.

It was very dark. Aside from the stars and the brilliantly lighted ship that towered above us, we could see nothing. Soon after we left the *Titanic*, the captain sent up rockets as a distress signal.

We all watched the ship steadily, except Master, who was asleep. Two hours later, we saw the last light go out and heard the dreadful cries that told us all was over. The great *Titanic* had gone down.

It seemed like a horrible dream. The heartbreaking silence and feeling of utter loneliness cast a deep gloom over our little boatload.

Toward three o'clock in the morning, an icy breeze sprang up and the sea grew rough. Master opened his eyes and said he felt seasick. But Muddie Boons, who had him on her lap, soon quieted him with a story of Cinderella.

About an hour later, someone suddenly shouted, "Here comes a ship!" Looking toward the horizon, we first saw a white light and then some rockets.

As the ship gradually approached, we feared she might either run us down or not see us at all, since we had no lantern. But soon she slowed down and then stopped.

As the faint mist cleared just before dawn, the new moon was setting, and a star was faintly twinkling on the pink horizon. The first rays of the sun cast a wonderful glow on the icebergs that rose from the ocean all around us.

Master suddenly opened his eyes and looking about him exclaimed, "Oh, Muddie, look at the beautiful North Pole with no Santa Claus on it."

A woman who had been crying smiled at him through her tears.

Our rescue ship, the *Carpathia*, looked very small amidst the few bits of wreckage where the huge *Titanic* had gone down. We finally drew alongside, and the men climbed aboard the *Carpathia* on rope ladders. The women were hauled up in a sort of swing, and the children in canvas bags.

The Carpathia raced through the night to rescue the Titanic's *passengers in the lifeboats.*

Soon everyone had been rescued — except for me. I lay alone in the empty lifeboat. Several minutes went by, but nothing happened. Everyone seemed to have forgotten me. My heart began to pound. I imagined being left there, tossed by the waves forever. Would I ever see Master again?

S uddenly I felt a terrible jerk, and then another. The boat swayed dangerously. I nearly fell into the icy water as several sailors pulled the lifeboat up to the decks of the *Carpathia*. I slid down the ribs of the boat, banging my back against each one along the way, and landed in a puddle.

"That's the last of them, then," said a sailor. He turned the boat over with a bang, and I fell onto the hard deck in a wet, miserable heap.

I lay there for what must have been hours. Then I heard a kind voice.

"Hello, there! Fancy seeing you again."

It was one of the
sailors from the *Titanic*. He
picked me up and squeezed
the water out of me, quite
taking my breath away.
Then he carried me down
some stairs and into a
warm room. It was full of
passengers with blankets
around them. Many of
them held hot drinks.

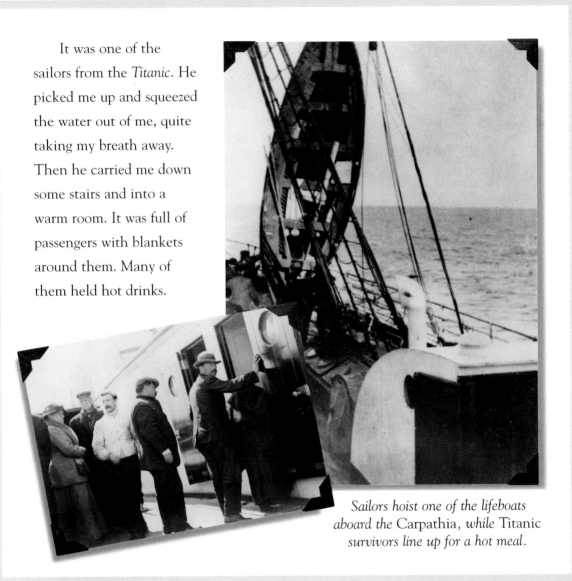

*Sailors hoist one of the lifeboats
aboard the* Carpathia, *while* Titanic
survivors line up for a hot meal.

*Douglas's father sent this telegram
from the rescue ship to relatives at home.*

"Polar!" a familiar voice shouted from across the room. It was Master. He rushed over and took me in his arms. I was delighted to see him again, too. But I was also rather upset to see that he was holding an ugly little brown bear. His mother had bought it for him in the ship's barbershop, thinking I had fallen overboard! As soon as Master saw me, however, he hugged and kissed me. He took me to bed with him that night and every night after, forgetting all about the other bear.

Survivors make clothes from blankets and comfort one another on the Carpathia.

D uring the next four long days, Master and I spent as much time as we could on deck, even though it was rainy or foggy every day. But the ship was so crowded, with more than seven hundred *Titanic* survivors as well as the *Carpathia*'s passengers, that there was hardly room to move. Master's mother and Muddie Boons spent hours cutting up blankets to make clothes for people who had none.

A three-year-old boy wears a night-gown made from one of the blankets.

At last we slowly steamed up New York Harbor in the middle of a thunderstorm. We were escorted by several boats full of people taking flash pictures of us.

"Look at the big parade, Muddie Boons, with no brass band!" Master cried as we saw the huge crowds of people and cars lining the docks. We were glad to escape the hubbub with members of the family who had come down to meet us.

I was happy to settle down to quiet country life in Tuxedo Park. The experience we had gone through seemed to bring Master and me closer together than ever before. He made a great pet of me and supplied me with two new suits of clothes and a little white wooden bed. I often thought back to how I was almost lost on the wide ocean. But I felt much better when Master tucked me beside him in bed each night and whispered softly in my ear, "Good night, Polar."

Master goes to school now, and I am left alone much of the time. But I always look forward to the warm greeting he gives me on his return. He has been a good Master, and I hope he will be blessed with a long and happy life. Though I realize that I shall see less and less of him as the years go by, I shall always feel, no matter what happens, that I occupy a large corner of his true and tender heart and that he will be loyal to me till the end. ❧

ACKNOWLEDGMENTS

Laurie McGaw would like to extend special thanks to Anthony Facciolo, who posed as the model for Douglas, and to her friend Sue Teeter, Anthony's mother. Thanks also to the following who posed as models for the illustrations: Ross Phillips, Gwynne Phillips, Patricia Moon Bartman (who also contributed her organizational skills), Deborah Gee, Norm Gee, Jennifer Gee, Cynthia J. Apitius, Kim Phillips, Gail Reddick, Scott Horner and Kevin Hancey. Thanks to Carol McGaw, Kathleen Phillips, George's Trains (Toronto), The Little Dollhouse Company (Toronto), Martin House Dolls and Toys (Thornhill, Ontario) and Moon Shadow Antiques (Badjeros, Ontario) for props; Deborah Gee, Cynthia J. Apitius and Hollywood Costumes (Thornhill, Ontario) for costumes; and Pat Billard for sewing Polar's outfits.

Leighton H. Coleman III would like to remember his grandparents, Mr. and Mrs. Leighton H. Coleman Esq., who had the foresight to preserve family treasures for the next generation. Thanks to Merri Ferrell for all her invaluable advice and assistance, and to Don Dirks for his tireless help. And, finally, thanks to Josh and Julie McClure of Island Color Photography for the wonderful reproductions of the archival photographs.

Madison Press Books would like to extend special thanks to Ken Marschall for his expert technical advice and inspiration in the creation of the *Titanic* paintings. We would also like to thank Don Lynch for his historical expertise. We are grateful to all those who have let us use their photographs: George Behe, Joe Carvalho, Jürgen Cieslik, Mr. George A. Fenwick, Mrs. B. Hambly, Otmar Dreher and Jörg Junginger of Margarete Steiff GmbH, Ed and Karen Kamuda of the Titanic Historical Society (P.O. Box 51053, Indian Orchard, Massachusetts 01151-0053), Don Lynch and Ken Marschall. And, finally, thanks to Dick Frantz, who identified Polar as a Steiff bear.

PICTURE CREDITS

All photographs are from the albums of Daisy Corning Stone Spedden unless otherwise stated.

Back cover: (Left) Ken Marschall Collection — 6: (Left) Collection of The New-York Historical Society (Right) The New York Public Library — 8: (Top) Kamuda Collection/The Titanic Historical Society — 18: (Top right) Mary Evans Picture Library — 20: (Left) Mary Evans Picture Library — 22: Mary Evans Picture Library — 26: Ken Marschall Collection — 28: (Top left) The Father Browne S.J. Collection (Top right) Joe Carvalho Collection (Bottom) Ken Marschall Collection — 31: (Left) George Behe Collection (Top right) Brown Brothers (Bottom) Ken Marschall Collection — 38: (Top) Ken Marschall Collection (Bottom left) Ken Marschall Collection (Bottom right) Brown Brothers — 41: (Left) Courtesy of Mr. George A. Fenwick (Right) The Titanic Historical Society — 42: Spedden family archives/J. Aidan Booth — 44: (Top left) Mary Evans Picture Library (Top right) Mary Evans Picture Library (Bottom) Mrs. B. Hambly Collection.

Illustrations © 1994, 1998 Laurie McGaw
Introduction © 1994, 1998 Leighton H. Coleman III
Text © 1992, 1994, 1998 Leighton H. Coleman III
Jacket, Design and Compilation © 1994, 1998 The Madison Press Limited

Originally published in the United States by
Little, Brown and Company
3 Center Plaza, Boston, Massachusetts 02108 U.S.A.

Published simultaneously in Canada by Little, Brown and Company (Canada) Limited and in Great Britain by Little, Brown and Company (UK) Limited.

First edition 1994. Revised edition 1998.

Library of Congress Catalog Card Number 94-75240

Canadian Cataloguing in Publication Data

   Spedden, Daisy Corning Stone, 1872-1950
   Polar, the Titanic Bear

   ISBN 0-316-80625-0 (hc)
   ISBN 0-316-80924-1 (miniature edition)

1. Spedden, Daisy Corning Stone, 1872-1950 — Diaries — Juvenile literature. 2. Titanic (Steamship) — Juvenile literature. 3. Shipwrecks — North Atlantic Ocean — Juvenile literature. I. McGaw, Laurie. II. Title.

G530.T6S64 1994   j910.91634   C94-931001-8

DESIGN AND ART DIRECTION
   Gordon Sibley Design
EDITORIAL DIRECTOR
   Hugh M. Brewster
PROJECT EDITOR
   Nan Froman
EDITORIAL ASSISTANCE
   Shelley Tanaka

PRODUCTION DIRECTOR
   Susan Barrable
PRODUCTION CO-ORDINATOR
   Sandra L. Hall
COLOR SEPARATION
   Colour Technologies
PRINTING AND BINDING
   Imago Productions, Hong Kong

POLAR THE TITANIC BEAR was produced by Madison Press Books, which is under the direction of Albert E. Cummings.

This Scholastic edition is only available for distribution through the school market.

Madison Press Books
40 Madison Avenue, Toronto, Ontario
Canada M5R 2S1

Printed in Hong Kong